To Stuart, with all my love

First published in 2018 by Child's Play (International) Ltd
Ashworth Road, Bridgemead, Swindon SN5 7YD, UK

Published in USA in 2018 by Child's Play Inc
250 Minot Avenue, Auburn, Maine 04210

Distributed in Australia by Child's Play Australia Pty Ltd
Unit 10/20 Narabang Way, Belrose, Sydney, NSW 2085

ISBN 978-1-78628-182-1
CLP220618CPL09181821

Printed and bound in Shenzhen, China

1 3 5 7 9 10 8 6 4 2

A catalogue record of this book
is available from the British Library

www.childs-play.com

Hide and Seek

Polly Noakes

Let's play
hide-and-seek!

One, two, three, four, five, six,
seven, eight, nine...

TEN!

Coming... ready or not!

I can hear you!

I'm sure
I can see you!

Are you up here?

Are you
down here?

Phew!
I can smell you!

Are you in here?

I know you're here somewhere!

Are you through here?

I give up!
It's my turn to hide now.
Come and find me!

Where can
she be?

Wait
a minute!
Who are you?

And where is she?

Surprise!